Chapter One

The THING in the Yard

I saw it the day we moved in.

As the removal men were leaving, I was on the pavement, checking out our new street. Across the road was a gateway with tall rusty gates.

PRIVATE KEEP OUT

Hmm – I wonder what's inside?

Before I had any ideas, the gates began to rattle. They swung back with a great screech to reveal something really bizarre. . .

3

A vintage Rolls Royce hearse with gleaming black paintwork and chrome! It glided out like a ghost. But as it swung into the street, its engine suddenly growled and it swept off into the night.

I rushed indoors to tell Mum, but she was far too busy unpacking pots and pans to do more than murmur, "Well, well." I don't think she took in what I was saying.

It wouldn't have mattered, except that three nights later it came back after midnight.

The thrum-thrum-thrum of its engine rattled my bedroom window and woke me. I leapt out of bed and peeped between the curtains.

The hearse had slid into the yard. The gates were already shut and two men, in long black coats, were opening the back of the hearse. They hauled something out. Something bulky.

I watched them carry a coffin into the big garage at the rear of the yard. The door swung shut behind them. I waited but nothing else happened. I yawned and went back to bed.

Chapter Two
SOME D.I.Y.

As soon as I woke in the morning, I checked from my bedroom window. There was no hearse in the yard. I went down to breakfast wondering if it had all been just a strange dream.

Mum, do people have funerals at midnight?

We are rather busy now, Howard.

My dad works on a cruise-liner. This trip, he'd been away for about a month and wasn't due home till the weekend. So Grandpa, the great D.I.Y. expert, was helping to get the place "shipshape".

He wanted to knock a wall down to turn two pokey rooms into one big bright one. Mum quite liked the idea, but had other things on her mind. She worked at home for a magazine called *Nature*.

To change the subject I told them about that hearse and the coffin.

I stared at him.

Leaving the cupboard in place, Grandpa got down from the steps, telling Mum she could rest her arms now.

Mum put her hand on my shoulder. "Howard, we've only just moved here. We want to make friends with our neighbours, not make up silly stories which they might not find very funny—"

CRASH!

The cupboard hit the floor. Grandpa gawped at it, puzzled.

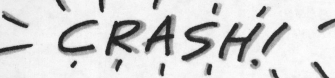

Chapter Three

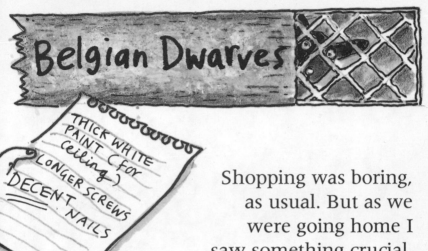

Belgian Dwarves

THICK WHITE
PAINT (for
ceiling)
LONGER SCREWS
DECENT
NAILS

Shopping was boring,
as usual. But as we
were going home I
saw something crucial.

I clenched my teeth and kept quiet until we were outside our house. I looked across to that yard and suddenly wished that we had never moved here.

Only bullies like Boris and Kevin would *play* with a bully like Terry.

I'd rather stay in and help Grandpa!

Mum tugged me across the road, and told the Cloanes about my interest in what went on in their yard. Terry's dad glared at me. His left eye twitched. He looked shifty, as if he realised that I had seen him last night, wearing his long black coat. I was certain now. I hadn't been dreaming.

"I'm sure I know you," Mum told him. "At least, I've seen you somewhere."

Worked down the supermarket. Cutting up meat. Got the sack. So now I'm dealing in pets... Let me show you.

He showed us a couple of hutches containing some miniature rabbits.

Belgian Dwarves. Kiddies love 'em!

Mum seemed to like them too. She said she might even buy me one, as soon as our house was in order.

Then Terry might like to drop in..?

"Right." Terry's dad tried grinning. "And your boy's more than welcome to mosey over here."

Mum promised to mosey me over as soon as we'd had our lunch.

Chapter Four

Food for Thought

Terry's mum was hard at work, shaping handfuls of minced meat to put through a hamburger press. She said she made all the burgers for BURGER BILL's in the High Street.

So we don't want your germs in here! Leave your shoes outside, please!

The kitchen was stuffed full of gadgets, and so was Terry's bedroom. He'd got his own brand-new computer. There must have been heaps of money in burgers and Belgian Dwarves.

Though, when we went out in the yard, Terry told me the rabbits were "rubbish".

Two hands gripped my shoulders. I have to admit it – I struggled.

Calm down, sonny!

Terry's dad reeked of sweat and horrible aftershave. "Terry's just trying to scare you. That shed's where we keep our pet foods – like oats for the Belgian bunnies."

Chapter Five

Food for Nightmares!

That evening I didn't say much, but nobody seemed to notice. Mum was unpacking china that no one would ever use. Grandpa was painting the staircase.

I could take it or leave it.

Grandpa tucked me into bed and sat down.

Three cannibals, Howard, remember? I was held in their vice-like grip. They pushed me towards an opening. Down below— Ooh my goodness!

A man-eating crocodile?

With jaws like garbage crunchers! End of the line I reckoned, unless I could do some quick thinking and—

Hold it, Grandpa. Cannibals eat human beings. Why didn't they want to cook *you*?

Grandpa looked a bit shifty.

It seems that the croc was their pet. They wanted to give him a treat so...

GULP!

Howard— are you sickening for something?

I was too sickened to answer. But once the light was out I was alone with my thoughts…

Then the window started to rattle. I knew the hearse was outside.

Chapter Six

BAD ★ ★ TO ★ ★ WORSE ★

This time I was wide awake. Here was my chance to find out what was REALLY happening in Terry Cloane's backyard. I got up and quickly pulled on some clothes.

Outside, I put on my trainers and scuttled across the street, dodging behind a parked car as Terry's dad pushed the gates shut. As soon as he'd turned away I hurried across and peered in – just in time to see a coffin being hauled out of the hearse. They carried it into the **foodstore**.

Had Grandpa been right from the start? Were the Cloanes body-snatchers? Were they getting supplies of corpses from the undertaker to feed to their...

Their WHAT?

This was stupid. The Cloanes were just yobbos, not ghouls. But they *were* up to something.

I flitted across the yard, dodging from hutch to hutch, keeping my eye on the doorway.

Lights were on in the foodstore. If I could get a peep in...

Too late. The door clanged shut moments before I reached it. All I could do was to eavesdrop.

I heard lots of huffing and heaving followed by a great thump and the clomp-clomp-clomp of footsteps.

I hid behind a bin as the door clanked open again. When I next looked, I saw Terry's dad and the big man casually shoving the coffin back into the hearse. It looked lighter. Because, it was empty now!

I had to hide again while Terry's dad locked up the store. Then they both went indoors, leaving me cold and shaky, ready to rush back home.

Chapter Seven

What Grandpa Says

I had to tell someone about this, and who would believe me but Grandpa? He was the one for *adventure*. Besides, his light was still on. I found him reading a thriller.

Grandpa—

Eh? Urgh-Uh? What's that, dear?

CANNIBAL ISLAND—

I tried to be calm and patient, but he was still half asleep. Grandpa couldn't take in what I said, so I dragged him across to my bedroom, but it was too late. The gates were shut, the hearse had gone, the yard was empty, and all the lights were out.

This might sound weird...

I started, but as I repeated it all, I knew it was worse than weird. Much, much worse. It was bedtime yarn stuff.

Grandpa scratched his beard.

We've got to be practical, Howard. If you were rearing young crocodiles, wouldn't you give 'em canned dog meat?

I saw his point. "But you told me that crocodiles liked human meat best . . ."

"Given the choice, but why spoil 'em? I take it you've SEEN these creatures?"

"Not . . . yet."

Grandpa tapped his nose . . . "How's this? It's more likely those nasty villains are grinding up their victims to make meat pies, or sausages . . ."

Or burgers!

"No, Grandpa, that's just being stupid."

Grandpa chortled. "So, crocs it is. Or tigers. I know when my leg's being pulled."

IT ISN'T!

I'd sleep on it, Howard.

Chapter Eight

What's in Store

Sleep on it? Thank you, Grandpa. I got no sleep that night and spent next morning yawning and getting in everyone's way.

I gave Grandpa an angry glare, but he winked at me like a pirate, as if we were sharing a joke. It made me determined to show him that I wasn't playing the fool.

I waited till after lunch, then took my life in my hands and went over to the Cloanes'.

Boris and Kevin were there, being egged on by Terry to boot a ball at the hutches to frighten the Belgian Dwarves.

I didn't like football. However, the door to the foodstore was goal, and while I was standing there waiting, I backed up really close. Close enough to hear some very odd noises inside. Eerie yacking noises. Then:

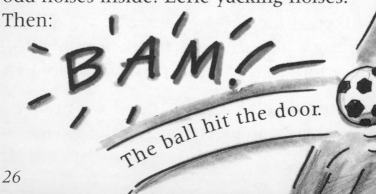

The ball hit the door.

GOAL!!!

The door to the foodstore **WHAMMED** open. Two hands slammed down on my shoulders.

You stop that, you'll wake the— Just **STOP** IT!

Pushing me out of the way, Terry's dad strode off to the house, leaving the door to the foodstore creaking on its hinges.

The three of them set to work, building a little fire to toast Terry's Action Man. They soon forgot about me.

Before I had really decided, I found myself walking backwards, through the door and into the foodstore.

What hit me first was the
stink – sort of swampy,
rotten and sour, like mud and
bad meat mixed up. I turned round,
holding my nose. My eyes
adjusted slowly...

A single lamp bulb, high up and
shrouded in webs, cast a dreary light
over a row of old bathtubs. Each one
of them was covered with a hefty sheet
of blockboard. I shuffled
towards the nearest,
dreading what I might find.
I lifted the board.

Pheweeh!

Less than a metre long, but it was a genuine croc. Terry *had* told me the truth!

I slammed the board down and moved on. I checked the other bathtubs. I counted nine young crocs. I felt all cold and shaky. What else was in this foodstore?

I found a big fridge with its door locked, and three small metal cages holding eight parakeets and one sad miniature monkey.

These weren't proper *pets*. Was this legal?
And what was that I could see?

At the back of the store was a workbench
with something bulky on top, covered
with a blanket.
Behind it, up on
the wall, was a
whole rack of
cleavers and
meat knives.

I'd seen enough. I stepped back, feeling
really queasy. That's when I trod on
something that bounced and squeaked.
I looked down.

I was standing on a large trapdoor. The sort that might cover up a vehicle inspection pit. Or maybe a dump for dead bodies? The smell was really disgusting.

Gripping the old iron ring, I heaved as hard as I could. The trapdoor suddenly shifted. Before I could see what was down there, it slithered up round my feet.

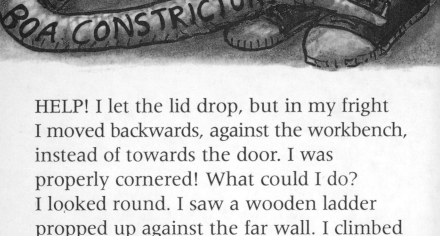

A THICK GREEN BOA CONSTRICTOR!

HELP! I let the lid drop, but in my fright I moved backwards, against the workbench, instead of towards the door. I was properly cornered! What could I do? I looked round. I saw a wooden ladder propped up against the far wall. I climbed to the top VERY FAST!

The snake coiled round the bottom of it. Could snakes climb ladders? The sort that lived in trees could!

Then I heard Terry's dad in the yard.

Stupid oafs! Put that fire out!

When he burst into the shed, I was almost glad to see him, but if he saw *me* he'd be furious. My mouth was dry. I waited. I watched as he unlocked the fridge.

Out came a polythene bag. It was crammed full of mushy pink lumps of . . . meat and grisly bones. He brought it across to the workbench and—

Hey, you! What you doing?

My heart lurched.

He lunged forward.

A hand gripped hold of the ladder, but with the other hand he…

… scooped up the snake by its middle.

Then he was dragging it backwards, tipping it into its pit and kicking the lid into place.

It happened so fast, I was gob-whopped! Without even meaning to, he'd saved me from boa-constriction. But I was still stuck up the ladder. So hold on. I had to be patient.

Terry's dad went back to his workbench. He pulled the blanket away. Underneath was a mincing machine.

He flicked a switch, the thing whirred, and soon he was cramming great handfuls of bloody, meaty gobbits into the funnel on top.

He filled the bowl, flicked off the switch, and sauntered from bathtub to bathtub, lifting up each board and scattering little pink morsels.

The crocodiles croaked like see-saws.

From my perch at the top of the ladder, I saw that it all made sense, in the most horrible way. Terry's dad was a maniac – grinding up human corpses to feed to his reptiles!

But worse was still to come.

Terry's mum came into the foodstore, clutching a mobile phone.

About tonight. It's your brother Ron.

She took the bowl from his hands, and he took the phone.

36

I was in such a panic I nearly slipped off the ladder. My heart was thunking away. Then the door slammed shut. Both the Cloanes had gone, taking the bowl of mince with them. Why? Too much for the crocs? Would she make the rest into burgers?!

I got out as fast as I could.

Chapter Nine

More D.I.Y.

Grandpa was in the hallway under considerable stress.

He had banged a nail through a floorboard and into a water pipe. Now a plumber was pulling up the boards, the hall was sopping wet, and Mum was mopping up water instead of working.

A minor setback here, Howard.

I kept my mouth shut until the pipe had been fixed. As soon as she'd paid the plumber, Mum stormed back to her desk, leaving Gramps holding the mop.

He looked a bit down, but I told him, trying to keep my voice low, what I had seen in that foodstore. And worse – what I'd overheard – about them fetching two foreign bodies.

Strangely, Grandpa nodded, as if it was all perfectly normal, and carried on swishing the mop.

Only two foreign bodies, you say?

Yes, Grandpa.

I got the message.

I'm serious, Grandpa!

I told him this wasn't a *yarn*. We had to find out, once and for all, WHAT WAS GOING ON IN TERRY CLOANE'S BACKYARD.

Tonight we must follow the hearse to see where it goes.

In my van?

If you could just do the driving...

You don't have to say you believe me.

He paused to stick a finger deep in one ear.

If you're wrong —if you make a fool of me, Howard—

I'll help with the wall. I'll clear up the rubble. How's that, Gramps?

He tugged at his beard.

That's a deal.

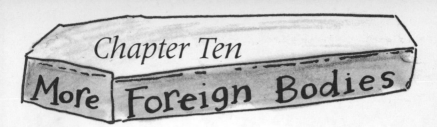

That evening I wasn't hungry, which was just as well because Mum had cooked **BURGERS** for tea.

urgh!

I went up to my room.
When I looked out of the window, across to that empty yard, I couldn't help wondering what would have happened to me, if Terry's dad had caught me in his so-called foodstore. I thought of those knives and cleavers, and all those meaty gobbits going into that mincing machine. I thought about crocs. And burgers.

41

In fact, I was very relieved when the time finally came for me to creep into Grandpa's room.

He wasn't. He made such a noise clomping down the stairs he woke up the dogs in the kitchen. But somehow we got to his van without Mum calling us back. She must have been dead to the world.

Unlike Terry's dad! He must
have been wide awake.
The moment I saw those huge
headlamps swing round
into our street, Terry's dad
whipped out of his
gateway, wearing his long
black coat. He swung
quickly into the
passenger seat.

KEEP
OUT

As the hearse glided off down the
street, Grandpa tried to start his van.

43

The engine coughed. It
even managed a splutter.
Then it cut out. Grandpa
cursed. He turned the key
again. The engine chortled
and hiccupped. He sat back
and whistled a bit.

The engine
humphed and
ha-ha-ha'd.
It choked, it
sniffed, it sneezed,
and, suddenly, it
roared like a lion.
The revs shot up.
The whole van shook. Then it backfired:

ε= BA-BA-BANG!

Lights went on in bedrooms all the way
down the street.

"That's got her," said Grandpa calmly.
He eased the old crate into gear, and
suddenly we were
away, lurching
round the corner
into an empty
High Street.

The lights were still red at the crossroads.
And there was the hearse. We'd been
lucky.

Red . . . Amber . . . Green. Off we went,
holding back from the hearse, but keeping
it in sight. We chugged along at thirty as if
we were off to a funeral, which was just
as well because Gramps was no whizz at
the wheel.

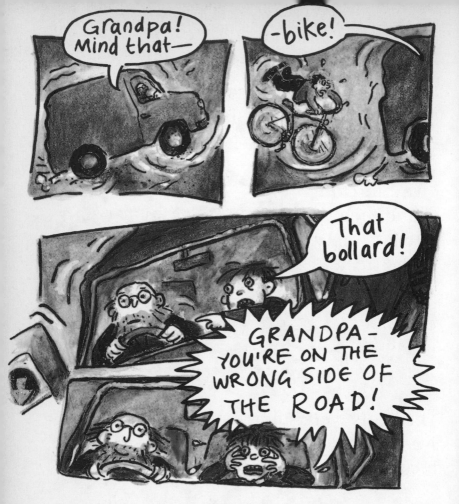

Thank goodness there wasn't much traffic. The hearse was keeping to side streets. After ten minutes or so, we left the last buildings behind. The road became narrow and pot-holed with blank walls either side. Grandpa said we were down near the docks.

The hearse swung off to the left,
into what looked like a scrapyard,
and Grandpa stopped the van a few
yards further down the road.

He was gripping my arm.

That's the dockfront.
we'd better
continue on
foot.

We didn't
dare use his
torch, so finding
our way wasn't
easy. Grandpa
bashed his knee.

Ssssh!

He hopped and limped. He kept on
grumbling away about how silly we'd feel
when we found the true explanation for
what those Cloanes were up to.

But somehow we reached the dockfront. We were close enough to the hearse to see by the light of its headlamps that something was still going on.

Two men we'd not seen before were counting a wad of money, while Terry's dad was busy, down on his knees, with the coffin. He pulled something out.

The thing hit the ground with a tinkle.

Now Grandpa was paying attention.
Leaning forward he fingered his beard.
And then, as if we'd agreed it, we both
started creeping closer. We sheltered
behind some old barrels. We watched as
they put on the lid and lifted the coffin to
slide it into the hearse.

The men hung
about until the
hearse was no more
than two red tail lamps
shrinking into the
night, then they
hurried across the
dockfront and
disappeared down
some steps.

49

We took a look over the edge. I could just see the shape of a boat sliding off into the gloom. I heard the phut-phut-phut of its motor.

Deckhands, off some foreign ship. I'll wager they've murdered a shipmate.

Two shipmates! And one more last night and —

I saw something glint on the ground. But Grandpa was already off, limping across the yard, muttering about keeping track of that coffin and bringing those villains to book. I put the tag in my pocket.

Chapter Eleven

Things go Wrong

Grandpa drove
like the clappers.
He got us back
so fast that we
were out of the
van in time to
glimpse the coffin
being lugged into the foodstore.

We waited. Mr Cloane and his brother
came out and went straight into the
house. Terry's dad was squawking away
about needing some coffee.

Time for
a decko.
Come on!

Grandpa squeezed between the gates into the yard. I followed.

The door to the kitchen was open. The Cloanes were jawing away. If they shut up for even a moment they'd hear Grandpa for sure. His every move made a LOUD SCRUNCH. But somehow we made it to the foodstore.

The light was on inside. It cast a cobwebby glimmer over the metal cages and old corroded bathtubs.

I lifted a board to show Grandpa and one of the crocs gave a croak. That didn't bother me now, but I kept Grandpa clear of the trapdoor which held the boa at bay. And when I saw the coffin, I was T E R R I F I E D !

It had been parked on the workbench, alongside the mincing machine. Grandpa made straight for it.

He must have been nervous too. I heard him clearing his throat. But he managed to lift the lid. He peeped in, coughed again, and glanced round at me.

Don't look, Howard.

As soon as he turned away I took a quick peep – couldn't help it. The bodies were covered with sacking. I saw Grandpa's hand inching forward. But as he lifted a corner, to pull the sacking away, something twitched underneath. It did.

It BULGED and HEAVED!

That body's **ALIVE!**

I lurched backwards, lost my balance and tumbled over. Before I could get up again, the door to the store crashed open. I heard Terry's dad.

Hey, you there!

You're trespassing. This is private property.

I rolled myself under the workbench, but Grandpa stood his ground.

"We're innocent," Ron protested.

"Pets are us!" Terry's dad cried.

Grandpa sort of humphed. He pointed his torch at the coffin and said, "I know what's in there."

Terry's dad waggled his chin. He licked his lips.

He swung round and pulled back the sacking.  **Oh, Gawwddd!** He dropped his torch, and then he was blundering round in all directions, cursing.

Howard, where are you hiding?

He hauled me out from under the work-bench. He lifted me up and told me to look in the coffin.
I held my breath and looked—

I saw two beautiful turtles.

So much for your FOREIGN BODIES!

Poor Grandpa had to apologize. I said I was sorry as well, but that didn't save me from getting an earful from Gramps in the yard. The Cloanes were both laughing their heads off...

I felt incredibly dumb – especially when we got home and found that we'd locked ourselves out. I had to ring the door bell.

Before he could say any more, Mum really let fly at poor Grandpa. She called him a silly old fool.

You're just like an overgrown schoolboy — playing at having adventures!

I had to own up, it was my fault.

But you must admit it was odd, Mum — fetching new pets in a coffin in the dead of night...

... as if they'd got something to hide. They did call them FOREIGN BODIES!

"Though, as it turns out," said Grandpa, doing his best to look stern, "the brother who drives the hearse, does work for the undertaker. But out of hours he helps Terry's dad with the pets."

PETS!

Mum exclaimed.

Mum gave us both a hard look.

But Mum stalked off into the kitchen.

As Grandpa and I swapped glances, not sure if we'd been dismissed, she stormed back holding out one of her *Nature* mags. She flicked through its pages.

I suddenly felt very tired.

Exotic
Pets...

Mum read out.

Endangered Species

Exotic Pets

Unscrupulous
dealers in pets
are smuggling
endangered
species includ-
ing monkeys
and rare
song-birds and
even dangerous
reptiles to sell
to rich collectors.
Some dealers
are making a
fortune...

She glared at us both. "Now do you get it?
I'm going to phone the police."

Chapter Thirteen

WELCOME HOME

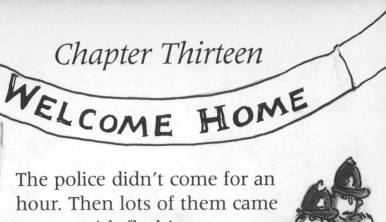

The police didn't come for an hour. Then lots of them came in two vans with flashing blue lights. They burst in through those metal gates, and barged straight into the foodstore. I watched from my bedroom window as they took Terry's dad away.

Next morning, some men from the zoo came, wearing protective gloves. The crocs were brought out in small cages and loaded into a van. The boa went in a big basket, labelled SNAKE – DO NOT OPEN. The crowd in the street were impressed.

Then things really did warm up, with people ringing our doorbell and asking us lots of questions…

We even got invited on to the Network TV News, along with an expert on reptiles. He said that the sad thing was:

I stuck my hand in my pocket and pulled out a slim metal tag.

This came off one of the turtles.

The reptile expert grabbed it and read out: "GALAPAGOS 194."

I don't want to blow my own trumpet, but he was over the moon.

This shows exactly where the turtles have come from — a special protected reserve on the Galapagos Islands — which means we can send them home!

So everything ended well – except for the Cloanes, of course. They didn't wait for the court case. They did a moonlit flit.

As for Dad, he came home late on Sunday morning – just as Grandpa was limbering up to take his first swing at that wall.